DARK HUNTER
WOLF TRAP

First published 2013 by
A & C Black, an imprint of Bloomsbury Publishing Plc
50 Bedford Square, London, WC1B 3DP

www.bloomsbury.com

ISBN 978-1-4081-8057-0

A CIP catalogue for this book is available from the British Library.

Printed and bound by CPI Group (UK) Ltd, Croydon CR0 4YY

1 3 5 7 9 10 8 6 4 2

WOLF TRAP

BENJAMIN HULME-CROSS

ILLUSTRATED BY NELSON EVERGREEN

A & C BLACK
AN IMPRINT OF BLOOMSBURY
LONDON NEW DELHI NEW YORK SYDNEY

The Dark Hunter

Mr Daniel Blood is the Dark Hunter.
People call him to fight evil demons,
vampires and ghosts.

Edgar and Mary help Mr Blood
with his work.

The three hunters need to be strong and
clever to survive...

Contents

Chapter 1

The Island

Mary, Edgar and Mr Blood sat in the small boat. A boatman was rowing them out to an island.

Mary could see the island in the distance. It looked like a scary, grey shadow in the white mist.

The Sheriff of the island had asked
Mr Blood for help. He said there was a
werewolf on the island. Mr Blood was a
famous werewolf hunter.

Mary was excited. *This is just the sort
of place to find a werewolf*, she thought.

Edgar was being sick over the side of
the boat.

"Cheer up, Edgar," Mary said.
"We're nearly there. Then the hunt for
the werewolf begins!"

"That doesn't make me feel better,"
groaned Edgar.

Mr Blood smiled at Edgar and Mary.
He was cleaning his crossbow.

The boatman did not speak. He had
said nothing all day.

"I have hunted many werewolves," said Mr Blood. "They are quite easy to kill. They are fast and fierce. But silver kills them at once."

He wiped down his silver-tipped arrows.

"You must be joking," said Edgar. "Werewolves are half human and half wolf. They are evil. They eat people alive. Maybe your silver arrows will kill them. But it won't be *easy*!"

"The thing about werewolves," said the boatman, "is that they can't swim."

Mr Blood, Mary and Edgar all turned and looked at him.

"I know that," said Mr Blood. "How do *you* know that?"

But the boatman didn't answer.

"Thank goodness!" said Edgar. "We're here."

They had reached a small harbour.

The boatman would not row right up to the beach. "You get out here," he said. "I will not go closer."

Edgar looked at the sandy beach. He gave a gasp of horror.

The beach was covered with bones.

Chapter 2

The Beach

"Mr Blood?" called a man on the beach. He was tall and dark-haired and he had a huge moustache.

"I'm the Sheriff," he said. "We have been waiting for you. I didn't know you would bring helpers. It is nice to see children here."

Mr Blood, Edgar and Mary jumped out of the boat and splashed through the water to the beach. At once, the boatman rowed away.

Edgar and Mary stared at the bones. The Sheriff laughed.

"A grim sight, isn't it?" he said. "We killed a lot of seals this summer. Let me take you up to the village."

They made their way up from the beach along a thin track. Mr Blood and the Sheriff walked ahead.

"Don't you think it's odd?" hissed Edgar to Mary. "Why did they leave bones all over the beach?"

"Maybe they haven't had time to clear up?" said Mary.

"Hmm," said Edgar. He thought something was wrong.

Mary and Edgar caught up with
Mr Blood and the Sheriff.

"We always find dead cattle the
morning after the full moon," the Sheriff
was saying.

"You have no idea who the werewolf
is?" Mr Blood asked.

"None at all," said the Sheriff.
"Sometimes, some people look a bit
red-eyed and wild. But we have no way
of knowing who is the werewolf."

"And have there ever been werewolves on this island before?" Mr Blood asked.

"Not as far as I know," the Sheriff replied.

"There will be a full moon tonight," said Mr Blood. "If you have a werewolf on the island, it will show itself. I will get rid of it by morning."

As they walked towards the village they heard the shriek of a seagull.

That sounds like a warning, thought Edgar.

Chapter 3

Bones

They went in the village inn. Mr Blood and the Sheriff sat at a table and made plans.

Edgar and Mary looked around. Hanging on the walls were lots of bones. There were dog skulls and deer horns, and shark jaw bones with razor-sharp teeth.

A serving maid called Anne came to talk to the Sheriff. She spoke quietly but Edgar and Mary could just hear what she was saying.

"They shouldn't be here," Anne said, pointing at Edgar and Mary.

"Sssh," said the Sheriff with a thin smile.

"This is no place for children," said Anne. "It's one thing to bring Mr Blood here. He is a werewolf hunter. It's his job to go into danger. But we all know what werewolves do to children."

The Sheriff's smile faded. He looked angry now.

Anne went on. "It's not right to put these children in danger. *They* aren't werewolf hunters. This is wrong."

"These people are our guests. Don't be rude," said the Sheriff crossly.

Anne stamped off and began mopping the floor.

"I don't like this," she said to herself.

"I'm going to talk to Anne," Mary told Edgar.

"Excuse me," she said to Anne.

"Yes, dear?" Anne looked up. She had a kind face.

"You don't need to worry about us,
you know," said Mary. "Mr Blood looks
after us."

Edgar laughed. He didn't think
Mr Blood looked after them very well.

"I'm sure he takes good care of you,
dear," said Anne. "It's a long time since
I've seen someone your age, that's all."

"There must be some children on the
island," said Mary.

Anne's eyes filled with tears and she
looked away. "There are no children. Not
any more," she said. "And you should not
be here now. It's not right."

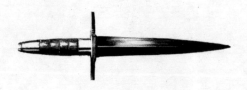

Anne looked sad and angry. "Go and sit with Mr Blood," she said. "Stay close to him."

Mary and Edgar walked back to the table and sat down.

"So, this is the plan," the Sheriff was saying. "I tell everyone to come to the barn before nightfall. We count heads every hour, to make sure nobody leaves."

"That's right," said Mr Blood.

"And we wait for the werewolf to change from human to wolf," said the Sheriff.

"Yes," said Mr Blood. "Werewolves have to turn into wolves on the night of the full moon. If you have a werewolf on the island, it will change shape tonight. And if everyone is in the barn, we will see it happen."

"And what will you do?" asked the Sheriff.

"I will kill it," replied Mr Blood.

Chapter 4

The Barn

About forty men and women came to the barn that evening.

Mary and Edgar stood at the back of the barn. The men and women kept turning to stare at them.

"I don't like this," Mary whispered to Edgar. "Why are there are no children here?"

"I know," said Edgar. "Something is wrong with this island."

The Sheriff called for everyone to listen.

"Friends! It is a full moon tonight." The Sheriff pointed at Mr Blood. "And we all know why this man is here."

"He kills werewolves," said a woman.

"He wants to kill one of us," growled one of the men.

Other men agreed with him. They didn't seem happy to see the Dark Hunter.

Mr Blood spoke up.

"You have nothing to fear from me unless you are hiding a very dark secret. Maybe there is a werewolf on the island. Maybe not."

A few people laughed.

"Tonight we will find out," said Mr Blood. "Is everyone on the island here?"

"We are all in this barn," replied the Sheriff.

"Good. Then lock the door, please, and hand me the key," said Mr Blood.

"Of course," said the Sheriff. His face twisted in a strange smile.

Edgar and Mary pushed through the crowd. They wanted to get to Mr Blood. The people gave them strange looks.

As they were making their way to the front, Anne blocked Edgar's way. He lost his balance and fell over.

Anne helped Edgar up.

As she took his hand, she slipped him a piece of paper. There was panic in her eyes.

Edgar guessed that she didn't want anyone else to see the note. So he closed his fist on it and walked on towards Mr Blood.

The Sheriff was trying to calm the angry people in the crowd.

Mary tapped Mr Blood on the arm. He leaned down.

"There are no children on the island," she hissed. "Did one werewolf kill them all?"

"I don't think so." Mr Blood looked worried.

Edgar looked down at the piece of paper. He gasped. He handed the note to Mr Blood. It was a warning.

This is a trap!

Get to a boat

as fast as you can

Save the children.

Chapter 5

Blood Moon

"I was afraid of this," said Mr Blood. "We need to escape."

"But what does it mean?" Mary asked. "I don't know what's going on."

"There is no time to explain now." Mr Blood was worried.

"There are some horses tied up outside the barn," said Mr Blood. "We'll need to take two horses and get back to the beach."

They turned back to face the crowd.

"Sheriff," said Mr Blood. "I am going to unlock the door to let the children outside. They are afraid of what will happen here."

The Sheriff's face was pale. His eyes seemed bigger than before.

"If you think that will help you," he growled. "Do as you wish."

Mr Blood unlocked the door.

All the people in the barn fell silent. Through the doorway Mary and Edgar could see a bright full moon. Its silver light shone down on the faces of the men and women. They all stood still.

It seemed as if the people were all waiting for something.

Only Anne moved. She pushed her way through the crowd with a hand over her eyes, and dashed for the door.

"Stop her!" shouted Mr Blood. He pulled out his crossbow.

"But she helped us," cried Edgar. "She wrote the note."

Anne made it to the door and ran out, into the moonlight.

As the light of the moon entered the barn, all the people fell to the ground.

They rolled around on the floor, wailing and growling.

Their shoulders began to swell. Arms grew longer. Legs grew shorter. Eyes burned yellow.

Human faces twisted into the faces of savage wolves.

"Quick!" shouted Mr Blood. "We must escape! They are *all* werewolves!"

Edgar, Mary and Mr Blood ran through the door. Mr Blood locked it behind them and bolted it with a large piece of wood.

"Edgar," snapped Mr Blood. "Take a horse, ride to the beach, and get us a boat. Mary, you ride with me. I'll need both my hands free."

He put an arrow into the crossbow as they got on their horses. The barn door shook as a werewolf tried to break it down.

Mr Blood, Edgar and Mary sped away on horseback. Behind them, in the barn, forty werewolves howled with rage.

Chapter 6

The Howling

They had ridden for less than a minute when they heard the barn door smash open.

The horses galloped for their lives. The howling grew louder.

Edgar heard a howl behind him
and turned to look. He saw Mr Blood
reload his crossbow. He had just shot a
werewolf.

Mary shouted at the horse to make it go faster.

As Edgar reached the beach, his horse reared up. Edgar fell off, and rolled on the sand.

A huge wolf stood between him and the boats. He waited for it to attack.

But the wolf just nodded its head towards the boats.

That werewolf is Anne! thought Edgar.

The wolf nodded at the boat again.
It was telling him where to go.

Of course, Edgar thought. *Werewolves can't swim.*

He ran to the nearest boat and began to drag it into the water.

Looking back, he saw the horse carrying Mary and Mr Blood skidding down the hill to the beach.

A pack of howling werewolves came after them.

Mr Blood shot another of his silver-tipped arrows. Another werewolf fell to the ground.

But there were too many of them.
He didn't have enough arrows to shoot
them all.

Mr Blood and Mary had only seconds
to reach the boat. They jumped off the
horse and ran across the sand to the
water's edge.

"You first, Mary!" yelled Mr Blood.

While Mary splashed into the water, Mr Blood loaded his crossbow and shot the nearest werewolf.

Then he turned and ran for the boat. But he tripped on a skull and fell.

A werewolf ran towards him and sprang up for the kill. But then another wolf flew through the air and attacked it. The two wolves began to fight.

"It's Anne," cried Edgar. "She is helping us!"

Mr Blood limped through the water and got into the boat. Edgar and Mary pushed the oars against the sand and the boat moved away from land.

The pack of werewolves reached the edge of the water, but they would not go further.

As the boat sailed off, Edgar asked
Mr Blood, "Why did they invite you to
the island?"

"They know I hunt werewolves," said
Mr Blood. "That's why they wanted to
kill me. They wanted to kill you and Mary
because werewolves eat children."

"So why did Anne save us?" said Mary.
"She was a werewolf too!"

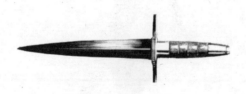

"She didn't want to hurt us," said Edgar. "She wasn't a monster like the rest of them."

"All werewolves are monsters," said Mr Blood. "But some monsters are worse than others."

The werewolves howled. The wild moon shone down on silver waves. Mr Blood, Edgar and Mary rowed out to the safety of the sea.